Read to me
Animal Tales

BYEWAY
BOOKS

Illustrations by:
SGA Illustration
Hadleigh, IP7 5AP

Illustrators:
Denise Elliott
Andrew Geeson
Sue King
Mary Lonsdale
Elizabeth Sawyer
Peter Wilkes

Designed and produced by
Autumn Publishing Ltd
Chichester, West Sussex

ISBN 1 85997 459 7

Printed in Spain

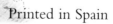

Contents

Puss in Boots

There once was a miller who lived in a mill with his three sons. The miller was very old and when he died the eldest son inherited the mill, the second son inherited the donkey, and the youngest son inherited the cat, Puss.

The youngest son was very disappointed to be left with Puss.

"What can I do with a cat?" he said, "I suppose I could have him made into a pair of furry gloves!"

On hearing this Puss said, "Please don't make me into gloves, I can help you become very rich, all I need is a pair of boots, a sack and some string."

The miller's son was surprised to hear the cat speak, but he gave him what he asked for.

Puss put the new boots on and took the sack and string. He put some grain in the sack and hid. After a while a group of hungry partridges came pecking at the grain. As soon as they hopped into the sack, Puss pulled the string tight and caught them.

He took the sack of partridges to the Palace. When he got there he bowed to the King and said, "My master, the Marquis of Carrabas, sends you these partridges as a gift." The King was pleased and gave Puss some gold coins.

"Take these
to your master
as thanks for his
generous gift."

Puss took the gold back to his master, and told
him the story.

From then on, Puss often took partridges to the
King and was richly rewarded each time.

One day, Puss in Boots heard that the King and
his daughter were going to take a drive by the river.
Puss and his master ran to the river.

"Take off your clothes and have a swim," said
Puss. The miller's son did as he
was told.

Puss could see the Royal coach
arriving and quickly
hid his master's clothes.
As the coach came
closer, Puss in Boots
cried out,
"Your majesty! My master
was swimming in the lake and a thief
stole all his clothes!"
The King immediately sent someone back
to the Palace to fetch some new clothes.
The clothes were of the finest cloth and
fitted him perfectly.
The miller's son joined them on their
drive. Puss ran on ahead and came to a
field where some farmers were working.
"Whose field is this?" he asked.
"It belongs to the Ogre," replied the farmers. Then
Puss said,
"When the King drives past tell him this field

belongs to the
Marquis of Carrabas."

Puss hurried on and came to a large cornfield and a magnificent forest. He told the people what to say when the King came by.

At last, Puss in Boots got to the Ogre's castle. He bowed before him and said, "I have heard that you can turn yourself into any animal. Can you turn yourself into a lion?"

"Easy!" said the Ogre and turned himself into a huge lion. "Brilliant!" said Puss. "I bet you can't turn yourself into something as small as a mouse."

"Watch this then!" roared the Ogre and turned into a mouse. But before he could turn himself back, Puss in Boots pounced on the mouse and killed it.

The King arrived at the castle and was very impressed with the Marquis of Carrabas. "Welcome to my master's castle, your Majesty!" said Puss in Boots.

The miller's son had fallen in love with the princess. He asked the King for her hand in marriage. The King agreed and they lived happily in the castle. When the King died, the miller's son became the new King, and Puss in Boots lived with his master in great luxury.

The Fox and the Grapes

Deep in the forest there lived a fox who was cleverer than most foxes. Everyone knows that a fox is cunning, but this fox was very clever too. It was not just that he could hide from any farmer and knew every tree and bush in the forest. This fox was especially clever because he believed in making the best of every situation he was in.

One day, the fox went out to raid the farmer's hen-run when a sparrow flew close behind. It was a very hot day and as the fox trotted across a field he came upon a bunch of ripe, juicy grapes which someone had dropped.

The fox had never eaten grapes
before but he nibbled at the bunch
and discovered that they were delicious
and cool.

"I am very lucky," he said aloud.
"Had it not been so hot I would
not have eaten the grapes, and then
I would never have known how
delicious they are!"

'Well," said the sparrow, who
was pecking at the ground
a few yards away,
"if you want to follow me
I shall be delighted
to show you where
that bunch of grapes
came from. Then you
can eat as many as you
please."

The fox thanked the sparrow politely, not knowing that the bird was about to lead him to a place where the grapes grew too high for him to reach.

"He won't boast about how lucky he is when he finds that he can't get at them," the bird said to himself, as he flew off in the direction of the grapevine.

"There they are, just as I promised," said the sparrow. The fox looked up at the grapes and jumped up to reach them, but try as he might he couldn't get them.

"What a pity they are so high!" cried the sparrow. But the fox shook his head.

"I see now that the grapes are unripe," he said. "How lucky I am that they are so high, otherwise I might have gobbled them up. Everyone knows that sour grapes are bad for you."

"Perhaps I'd be happier too if I stopped wanting things I can't have," thought the sparrow.

From that time on, the sparrow became the fox's friend and was a much happier little bird.

The Ugly Duckling

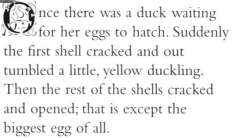

Once there was a duck waiting for her eggs to hatch. Suddenly the first shell cracked and out tumbled a little, yellow duckling. Then the rest of the shells cracked and opened; that is except the biggest egg of all.

She gathered the ducklings to her and looked at the big egg. Why was it taking so long to hatch? Then a crack appeared in the shell and there stood the biggest and ugliest duckling.

"Come along, children," said the mother duck. "Come and learn to swim."

Off they went to the river.
Soon they were all swimming
happily after their mother. But
the ugly duckling, who swam
best of all, stayed at the back
as everyone picked on him.

Then mother duck took
her family to the farmyard
and said,
"This is where we live. Keep
away from the cat and be
polite to the big rooster."

Everyone in the
farmyard greeted the
ducklings, but when they saw
the ugly duckling they laughed
and called him names, he felt
very sad and lonely.

The ugly duckling was so unhappy
he ran away. He hid in the reeds by
the river and cried.

The following day he set off
across the fields and came to a cottage.
The old woman who lived there found
him huddled on the doorstep and took
him in. But the old woman's cat hissed
at him because he could not catch
mice, and the hen pecked at him
because he could not lay eggs.

One day he looked up and saw
some swans flying overhead.
"Oh, they are so beautiful. I
wish I could be like them. I'm
sure nobody laughs at them, or
calls them names."

The summer was over and the cold weather came. One day it was so cold that the water on the pond froze around the duckling as he was swimming. He saw a woodcutter and gave a feeble quack, the man went over to the pond.

The woodcutter quickly broke the ice and picked up the ugly duckling and took him home. At his cottage he wrapped up the ugly duckling to keep him warm and told his children to look after him.

The children loved their pet and they fed the ugly duckling and kept him warm. When he had thawed out they played with him, he was quite

clumsy and it did not take long before he was in disgrace for knocking things over. The children's mother said he could not stay in the house so he ran away again and hid.

At last spring came, with soft breezes and warmer days, and the ugly duckling decided it was time to leave his safe hiding place.

The ugly duckling spread his wings and discovered he could fly. He flew high above the countryside and, looking down, he saw three swans swimming on a lake. He had watched them the previous year, when he had been running away.

The swans looked up and called
to him to join them. Hardly daring
to believe that anyone would want to
know him, he flew down.

As he landed on the lake he saw
his reflection in the water and joyfully
exclaimed,
"I'm a swan! I'm a swan!"

The Hare
and the Tortoise

All the animals were having a discussion, and agreed that the hare was the fastest creature in the forest. "How swiftly he runs!" the other animals would say.

Now, the slowest creature was the tortoise, for as everyone knows, the tortoise is a very slow-moving fellow indeed.

One day the hare
met the tortoise and waved
a greeting.
"It must be dull being so slow. Don't
you ever think what fun it would be
to run as fast as me?"
"Well, no, I can't say I do," the tortoise
told the hare. "After all, you must remember
that I carry my house on my back, and it's
very heavy. But you'd be surprised how
quickly I get from one place to another,
just plodding along." And he closed his
eyes because he felt like a nap.
"Quickly!" exclaimed the hare
with a laugh. "Whoever heard
of a tortoise moving quickly!"
The tortoise opened his eyes.
"I can see you don't

believe me," he said. "If you like, we can have a race and then you'll find out just how fast I am."

"A race!" the hare laughed. "You want to have a race with me?"

"Yes," said the tortoise.

The news spread through the forest quickly, and soon a starting line and a finishing point had been chosen.

"Ready, steady, GO!" shouted the badger, and the hare sped off, with his paws thumping over the ground. The tortoise plodded along just as he always did and, by the time the hare was out of sight, the tortoise had covered only a short distance.

"This is the last time I race anyone

as slow as the tortoise," the hare said. It was warm in the sun and he felt sleepy, so he settled down under a tree and closed his eyes and fell asleep.

When he awoke, there was no sign of the tortoise. He began to run but when he came in sight of his rival he was amazed to see that the tortoise was only a little way from the finishing point.

"I must hurry!" gasped the hare. But try as he might, the tortoise had got too far ahead and crossed the finishing line first.

"As I was explaining," he said to the hare, "I may not be very fast, but I never stop. Slow but sure wins!"

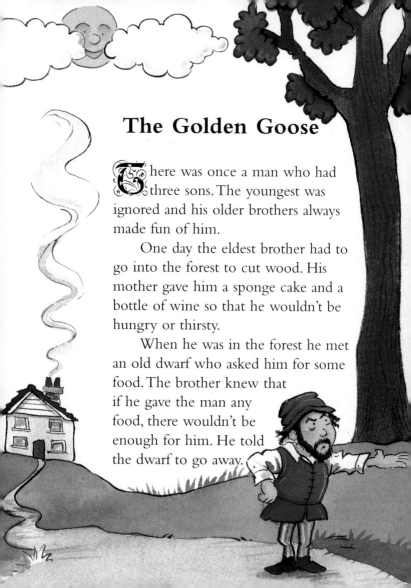

The Golden Goose

There was once a man who had three sons. The youngest was ignored and his older brothers always made fun of him.

One day the eldest brother had to go into the forest to cut wood. His mother gave him a sponge cake and a bottle of wine so that he wouldn't be hungry or thirsty.

When he was in the forest he met an old dwarf who asked him for some food. The brother knew that if he gave the man any food, there wouldn't be enough for him. He told the dwarf to go away.

He started to chop the tree but he missed and the axe cut his arm, and he had to go home. This had been the old dwarf's doing.

So the second son went into the forest and, like his brother, he met the dwarf who asked for food. He replied the same way as his older brother. It was not long before he too was punished. He cut his leg and had to be carried home.

Then the youngest brother said, "Father, let me go and cut wood."

"Your brothers have both been injured. You will hurt yourself," said his father.

But the boy begged and begged until his father gave in, "Go then, you may learn from your mistakes."

The boy's mother gave him a cake that had been cooked with water and in ashes, and a bottle of sour beer. When he was in the forest he also met the old dwarf.

The dwarf greeted him and said, "Give me a piece of your cake and a drink, I am so hungry and thirsty." "I have only a plain cake baked in ashes, and sour beer," he told the dwarf. "But if you find it to your taste, we will share it."

When he unwrapped his plain cake it had become a fine

sponge cake and the beer was a good wine. They ate and drank and the dwarf said,

"You are very kind so I will bring good fortune to you. See that old tree there, go and cut it down, and you will find something in the roots."

Then the little man disappeared.

The youngest brother went to the tree and cut it down. When it fell, a goose with feathers of pure gold was sitting there. He took the goose with him and spent the night at an inn. The innkeeper had three daughters and when they saw the goose, they wanted one of its golden feathers.

The eldest girl thought to herself, "I am sure I can have just one feather."

When the young man left the room, she seized the goose by the wing but her hand stuck to it. Then the second daughter tried to take a golden feather. But as soon as she touched her sister, she got stuck too. Finally, the youngest girl tried. But before she realised, she too was stuck fast.

The next morning, the young man put the goose under his arm, and set out without a thought for the three girls who were still hanging on. They had to follow him everywhere.

A parson saw the procession and said to the three girls,

"Shame on you, you disgraceful girls! Why are you chasing this lad through the fields?"

With these words, he tried to pull the youngest by the hand. As soon as he touched her, he too got stuck and had to run behind.

As they went on their way they saw two peasants working in a field. The parson was calling out to them, begging them to cut him free. However, the moment they touched him they stuck to him and now there were six people running behind the young man and his goose.

Next, they came to a city where the King had a daughter who was so sad that nobody could make her laugh. He proclaimed that whoever made her laugh could marry her. The young man heard this, and appeared before the Princess. When she saw all the people running after him and his golden goose, she burst out laughing. She laughed and laughed, and couldn't stop.

So, the young man asked the Princess to become his wife. The King could not refuse and they were

married. When the King passed away, the young man and his Princess became the new King and Queen and lived happily ever after.

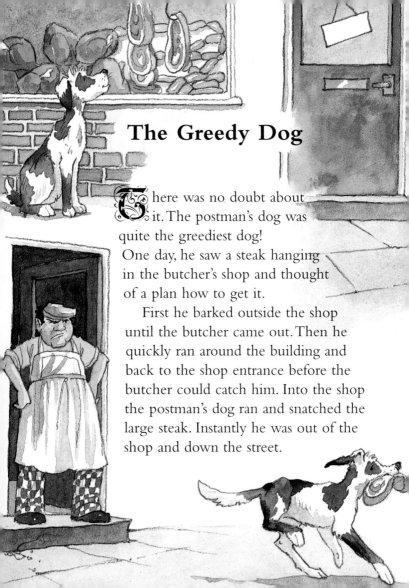

The Greedy Dog

There was no doubt about it. The postman's dog was quite the greediest dog! One day, he saw a steak hanging in the butcher's shop and thought of a plan how to get it.

First he barked outside the shop until the butcher came out. Then he quickly ran around the building and back to the shop entrance before the butcher could catch him. Into the shop the postman's dog ran and snatched the large steak. Instantly he was out of the shop and down the street.

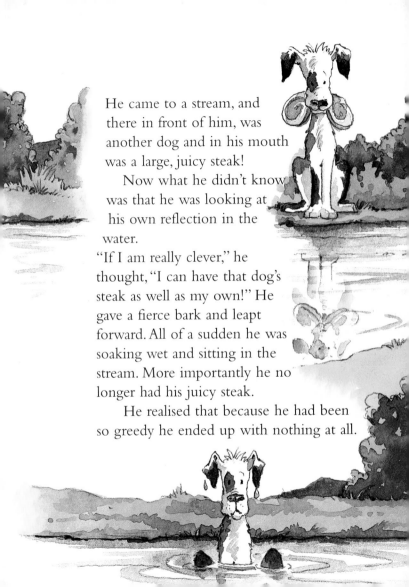

He came to a stream, and there in front of him, was another dog and in his mouth was a large, juicy steak!

Now what he didn't know was that he was looking at his own reflection in the water.

"If I am really clever," he thought, "I can have that dog's steak as well as my own!" He gave a fierce bark and leapt forward. All of a sudden he was soaking wet and sitting in the stream. More importantly he no longer had his juicy steak.

He realised that because he had been so greedy he ended up with nothing at all.

The King
of the Birds

One day, all the birds that
could fly, decided one of
them should become king.
But how would they choose
which bird it would be?
"The only way to decide is by
a contest. The bird that can fly
the highest every day for
five days will be king," said
the eagle, knowing that he
would be able to fly the highest
for five days.

On the first day of the
contest all the birds gathered.
Hiding in a tree was a tiny wren.

The signal sounded for the start of the contest and all the birds flew up into the air. The tiny wren was so small it had managed to hide in the eagle's feathers.

Most of the birds didn't last very long in the contest and on the last day of the contest only the eagle was left. He called out, "I've won, I've won! No one has flown higher than me." "Except me," sang the wren, who was now flying above the eagle. The other birds were amazed by the tiny bird's strength, and they declared the wren to be king of the birds.

The Musicians of Bremen

There once was a farmer who owned a donkey that worked very hard. But one day the farmer decided the donkey was too old to work any more.

The donkey knew what the farmer was thinking so he left. "I'll go to Bremen and become a musician," he thought.

On his journey he came across a tired dog and an unhappy cat lying at the side of the road. The donkey asked them what was wrong. The dog and cat explained that their

master was going to sell them, as they were too old to work. They had decided to run away together. "Come with me to Bremen, I am going there to make a living as a musician," said the donkey.

The dog and cat thought this was a good idea and joined him.

The three of them then came across a farmyard. Sitting on a fence was a cockerel crowing at the top of his voice.

"Why are you crowing now? Dawn was ages ago," said the donkey.

"I am crowing while I still can," the cockerel replied. "My mistress is having guests for dinner, she wants to make me into soup!"

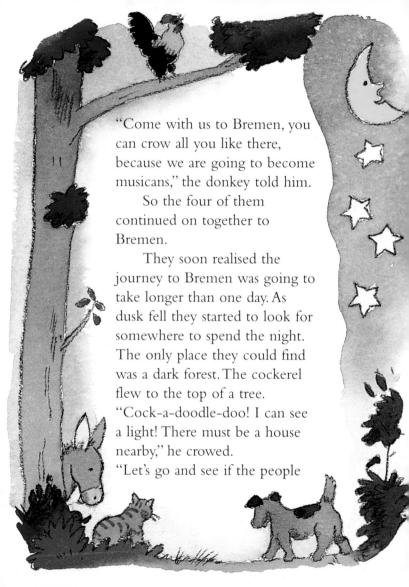

"Come with us to Bremen, you can crow all you like there, because we are going to become musicans," the donkey told him.

So the four of them continued on together to Bremen.

They soon realised the journey to Bremen was going to take longer than one day. As dusk fell they started to look for somewhere to spend the night. The only place they could find was a dark forest. The cockerel flew to the top of a tree. "Cock-a-doodle-doo! I can see a light! There must be a house nearby," he crowed.

"Let's go and see if the people

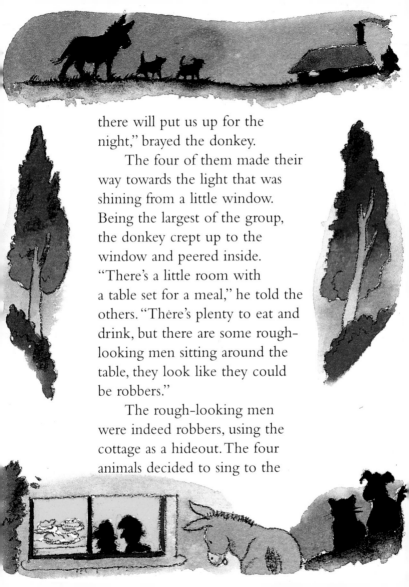

there will put us up for the
night," brayed the donkey.

The four of them made their
way towards the light that was
shining from a little window.
Being the largest of the group,
the donkey crept up to the
window and peered inside.
"There's a little room with
a table set for a meal," he told the
others. "There's plenty to eat and
drink, but there are some rough-
looking men sitting around the
table, they look like they could
be robbers."

The rough-looking men
were indeed robbers, using the
cottage as a hideout. The four
animals decided to sing to the

men, so that they might be invited in.

The dog jumped on the donkey's back, the cat sat on the dog's shoulders and the cockerel flew onto the cat's head. Then the donkey brayed with all his might, the dog barked, the cat miaowed, and the cockerel crowed so loudly that the cottage shook. The sound was almost deafening, the terrified robbers stopped eating and looked at the window.

The donkey accidently broke the window which frightened the robbers so much that they ran out of the house into the forest.

The donkey, dog, cat and cockerel sat down at the table and tucked into the food.

When they had eaten everything
they thought they would stay the
night and they all fell asleep.

At midnight, the robbers met
in the forest to decide what they
should do. The leader said to the
youngest robber,
"We need to know what is
happening in the cottage. Go and
look to see what is going on."

The young robber did not
want to go, but as he was under
orders he had no choice. He crept
round the cottage, and as it was
quiet, he went inside. It was dark,
so he needed to light a lamp.

He saw something glowing in
the hearth which he thought was
coal. He went to light a twig from

the hot embers. They were in fact the cat's eyes glowing in the hearth, and when he poked the stick at her, she hissed and scratched his face.

The robber tried to run out of the cottage, but he tripped over the dog. The dog growled and caught hold of the robber's trousers with his teeth. The robber tore himself free and ran outside, where the donkey was sleeping. The donkey woke with a start and kicked his back legs up in fright.

All this noise woke the cockerel in the rafters, and he crowed at the top of his voice, "Cock-a-doodle-dee!"

The scared robber thought he heard, "Kick him up to me!" He ran into the forest,

where he told the others,
"There's a witch in our cottage –
look how she scratched my face.
She's got some servants and one
was guarding the door, he tore a
piece from my trousers! And when
I got outside, a couple of them
beat me with sticks, and one of
them on the roof shouted,
'Kick him up to me!' "

The robbers decided not to go
back to the cottage and ran away as
fast as they could.

The donkey, dog, cat and
cockerel liked the cottage so much
that they decided to stay there
forever. They sang from time to
time for their own pleasure and
lived very happily together.

The Fox and the Stork

There was a fox who was fond of playing tricks on people. But his tricks were not always funny to others.

One day the fox asked a stork to dine with him, and the bird gladly accepted.

The stork arrived for dinner and the fox brought out two plates of fish stew. When the stork saw this he knew the fox had tricked him. He couldn't eat with his long, thin beak.

"Eat up," said the fox.

"I'm afraid I'm not very hungry,"

said the stork. So the fox had both plates of stew.

"But do have dinner with me tomorrow," said the stork.

The fox arrived at the stork's house.

"I have made a special meat stew for you," the stork said.

He put a bottle, with a long neck, full of steaming stew in front of the fox. The hungry fox licked all around the neck but he couldn't get at a single drop of stew. He watched the stork eat his dinner easily.

"I thought it was funny when I tricked the stork, but now I realise it wasn't," said the fox to himself.

Androcles and
the Lion

Many years ago in a land far away there was a slave named Androcles. Life as a slave was terrible, and many slaves tried to escape, but if they were caught they were thrown to the lions.

Androcles managed to escape and he hid in a nearby forest. He came across a lion lying down and obviously in great pain. Androcles was scared and began to run away. But he realised the lion could not chase him,

and he went to see what was wrong.

As he approached the lion it stretched one of its front legs towards him. The paw was swollen and bleeding. Androcles could see a huge thorn sticking in the paw that was causing the pain.

Androcles pulled the thorn out and bandaged the paw. The lion was very grateful and stood up and licked Androcles's hand, as though he were a faithful dog rather than a fierce lion.

Androcles and the lion parted company the best of friends. But one dreadful day Androcles was recaptured and sent to prison.

Androcles was led into the arena, and the lion released. It ran towards Androcles roaring, and he was terrified. But as soon as it got close to Androcles the lion recognised him! The lion had also been

captured. Instead of harming Androcles the lion just licked him.

The crowd was amazed. The Emperor summoned Androcles and made him tell the whole story.

Androcles and the lion were freed. They decided they would always stay together.

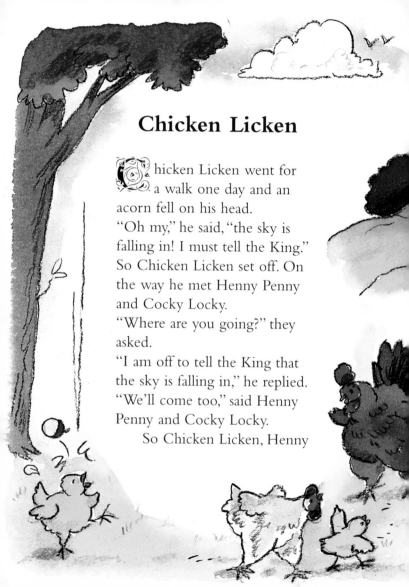

Chicken Licken

Chicken Licken went for a walk one day and an acorn fell on his head.

"Oh my," he said, "the sky is falling in! I must tell the King."

So Chicken Licken set off. On the way he met Henny Penny and Cocky Locky.

"Where are you going?" they asked.

"I am off to tell the King that the sky is falling in," he replied.

"We'll come too," said Henny Penny and Cocky Locky.

So Chicken Licken, Henny

Penny and Cocky Locky set off
to see the King.

On the way they met Ducky
Lucky and Drakey Lakey.
"Where are you all going?"
"We are off to tell the King that
the sky is falling in!" they said.
"Then so will we," said Ducky
Lucky and Drakey Lakey.

So Chicken Licken, Henny
Penny, Cocky Locky, Ducky
Lucky and Drakey Lakey all set
off together.

Next they met Goosey
Loosey and Turkey Lurkey.
"Where are you all off to?"
Chicken Licken told them they
were going to see the King, and

Goosey Loosey and Turkey Lurkey decided to go too.

So Chicken Licken, Henny Penny, Cocky Locky, Ducky Lucky, Drakey Lakey, Goosey Loosey and Turkey Lurkey set off to see the King.

On their journey they met a cunning fox.

"Where are you all going?" asked Foxy Loxy.

"The sky is falling in and we are on our way to tell the King!" they cried.

"Then follow me," said Foxy Loxy, "I know the way."

So Chicken Licken, Henny Penny, Cocky Locky, Ducky

Lucky, Drakey Lakey, Goosey Loosey and Turkey Lurkey followed Foxy Loxy.

But instead of taking them to see the King, he took them to his den, where he ate them all for his dinner.

The foolish birds didn't get to see the King and, of course, the sky never did fall in!

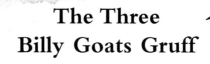

The Three
Billy Goats Gruff

Once upon a time there were three
billy goats called Gruff. They lived
together in the mountains and spent the
days happily eating lush green grass by the
river.

One day the three billy goats Gruff
stood by the river and looked across to
the other side. They saw really fresh, green
grass, and they decided to find a way to
cross the river. They trotted along and
finally came to a wooden bridge.

"The bridge does not look very strong," said the smallest goat. "I'll go first to see if it is safe."

Under the bridge lived a wicked troll. When the smallest goat went clip-clopping across, the troll peeped out from under the bridge, "Who's that clip-clopping over my bridge?" roared the troll. "I'll eat you for my dinner!"

The small goat replied, "You don't want to eat me, I am small and bony, my brother is bigger and will be tastier to eat."

The troll was greedy, so he let the little goat cross the bridge to the fresh, green grass on the other side.

The middle-sized goat began

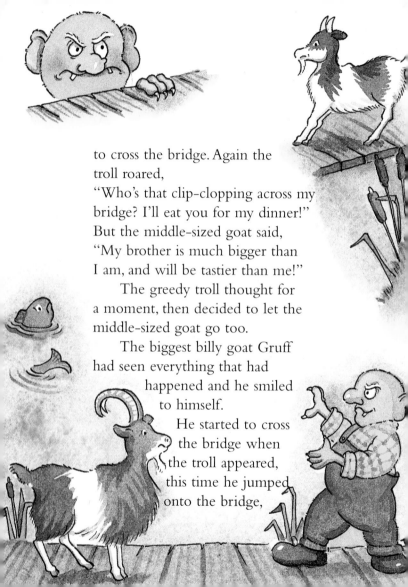

to cross the bridge. Again the
troll roared,
"Who's that clip-clopping across my
bridge? I'll eat you for my dinner!"
But the middle-sized goat said,
"My brother is much bigger than
I am, and will be tastier than me!"

The greedy troll thought for
a moment, then decided to let the
middle-sized goat go too.

The biggest billy goat Gruff
had seen everything that had
happened and he smiled
to himself.

He started to cross
the bridge when
the troll appeared,
this time he jumped
onto the bridge,

"Who's that clip-clopping across my bridge?" roared the troll.
"I will eat you for my dinner!"
"I am the biggest billy goat Gruff," he replied and with that he lowered his horns and charged at the troll. With a great roar, the troll flew up into the air and down into the river below. The current was so strong, that the water carried him away, never to be seen again.

The three billy goats Gruff lived happily eating the fresh, green grass and crossed the bridge whenever they liked.

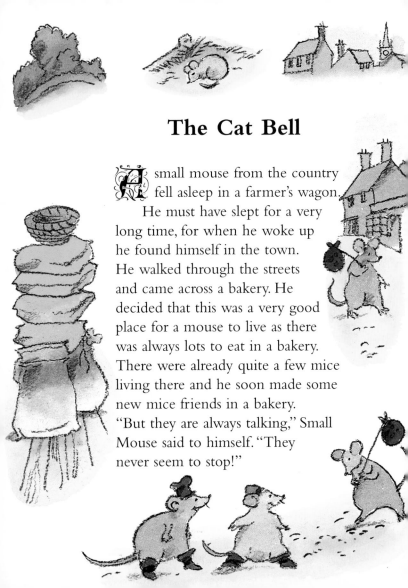

The Cat Bell

A small mouse from the country fell asleep in a farmer's wagon. He must have slept for a very long time, for when he woke up he found himself in the town. He walked through the streets and came across a bakery. He decided that this was a very good place for a mouse to live as there was always lots to eat in a bakery. There were already quite a few mice living there and he soon made some new mice friends in a bakery. "But they are always talking," Small Mouse said to himself. "They never seem to stop!"

"Come along, Small Mouse," they would cry, "haven't you anything to say?"

Small Mouse would smile and shake his head and protest that the mice, where he came from, weren't great talkers.

Then one terrible day, the baker bought a cat.

"I've seen it! I've seen it!" panted a very frightened mouse, as it scuttled back into the safety of the hole. "It's undoubtedly a cat. A huge one with great green eyes, long whiskers and fierce claws –", the poor mouse shuddered.

This was really something that needed to be discussed! The mice sat down and talked for hours.

At last the wisest bakery
mouse cried,
"I have the answer!" Everyone paid
attention.
"We must put a bell around the
cat's neck. Then we will be able
to hear him coming."
"What a good idea!" the mice
cried. "You are clever! And since
it was your idea, you would tie the
bell on best."
"Oh, I'm far too old," said the
wise mouse hurriedly.
None of the other mice wanted
the job either. At last Small Mouse
said,
"I know I am only a country
mouse and not as clever as you,

but why don't we move next door?
The wife of the pastry cook doesn't
like cats, so we will be quite safe."
     The bakery mice were
delighted at the idea.
"However did you think of that?"
they cried.
"In the country we simple mice
aren't used to talking, like you town
mice. We just get things done,"
Small Mouse answered modestly.

Sly Fox and Little Red Hen

Once upon a time, in a tiny house in the wood, there lived a Little Red Hen. She lived near a Sly Fox.

One day, as the Little Red Hen was in the wood collecting sticks, the Sly Fox crept into her house and hid. When she returned home, Sly Fox jumped out at her!

The Little Red Hen flew up to the rafters. Sly Fox laughed, "I've got you now!" as he started running round and round in a circle.

She watched as he went faster
and faster, soon she was so dizzy
she fell down. Sly Fox put her
in a sack and set off for home.

On his way he had a nap.
While he was asleep, Little Red
Hen crept out of the sack and
filled it with stones.

When Sly Fox woke from
his nap he picked up the sack
and carried on with his
journey. He arrived home and
boiled some water. He then
emptied the sack into the
boiling water. The stones
splashed the Fox and gave him
such a fright that he ran away,
leaving the Little Red Hen to
live happily ever after.

The Mouse and the Lion

A mouse had been caught by a lion. The mouse pleaded, "If you let me go, some day I shall help you in return." The lion did not know how a mouse could help him, but he decided such a small mouse would not make a very good meal so he let the creature go.

One day some hunters set a trap, and the lion was caught. He was lying helpless within a strong net, when he heard

a tiny voice say,
"I have come to free you."
The mouse began to gnaw through
the rope. It was not long before he
had chewed right through the rope
and the lion was freed.
"How can I ever repay you?" asked
the lion.
"Don't you remember? I am the little
mouse you set free. One good turn
deserves another. I am doing you
a good turn, just as I promised."

The Three Little Pigs

Once there were three little pigs who decided it was time to leave home.

They set off to find new homes. When they had been walking for a while, they saw a man with a cart full of straw.

"I could build a house with straw," said the first little pig.

So he bought the straw and built his house.

Next the two remaining little pigs met a man who had a cart of sticks.

"With those sticks I could build myself a fine house," said the second little pig.

So he built his house with sticks.

The third little pig walked further up the road, where he came across a man with a cart full of bricks.

"With those bricks I could build a fine, strong house," said the third little pig.

So he bought the bricks and built his house.

That night the first little pig heard a voice outside his door – it was a big, bad wolf!

"Little pig, little pig, let me in!"

"No, no, not by the hair of my chinny chin chin, I will not let you in!" said the little pig.

"Then I'll huff and I'll puff, and I'll blow your house down!" The wolf huffed and puffed and blew the house of straw down.

The little pig ran to his brother's house made of sticks.

The next night the two little pigs
heard the wolf's voice,
"Little pigs, little pigs, let me in!"
"No, no, not by the hair on our
chinny chin chins, we will
not let you in!" said
the pigs.
"Then I'll huff and I'll puff
and I'll blow your house
down!"
So the wolf huffed and
puffed and he blew the
house down.
The two frightened
little pigs ran to their
brother's house made of
bricks. That night they heard
the wolf's voice again.
"Little pigs, little pigs, let me in!"
"No, no, not by the hair on

our chinny chin chins, we will not let you in!" cried the pigs.

"Then I'll huff and I'll puff and I'll blow your house down!"

So he huffed and he puffed but the house stayed standing. The wolf was very cross and he said,

"I'm coming down the chimney to get you!"

The three little pigs put a pot of boiling water on the fire. As the wolf leapt down the chimney he landed in the water!

The wolf jumped out of the pot and ran out of the house howling in pain and never to be seen again.

The Man Who Spoke to Animals

Once there lived a young man called Joseph, who was poor and had no money to buy food. On his travels he found a snake, which he killed, roasted and ate. It tasted wonderful and when he finished eating he discovered he could hear animals talking.

The following day Joseph came across three fish that had been caught in a net.

"Free us, throw us back into the water," they pleaded.

He threw them back, as they asked, and in return

the fish promised to help him one day.

The following day he heard lots of small voices calling up to him. "Mind where you step, don't tread on us!" He looked down and saw some ants in the path. He stepped aside to let them pass.

"Thank you. If we can help you one day, we will," they said.

Joseph continued on his journey and came across three young ravens that were too small to feed themselves. They cried, "Feed us, or we will die."

He found them some food, and they too promised to help him.

A few days later he heard some people talking about the King who was looking for a husband

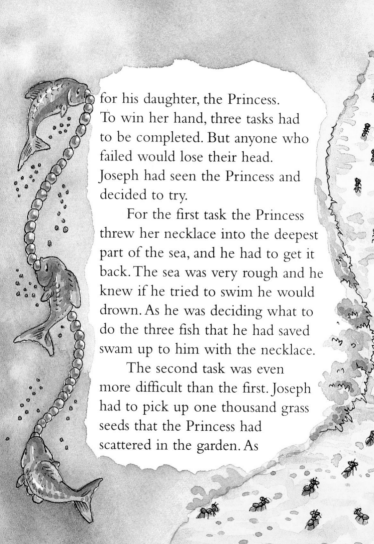

for his daughter, the Princess.
To win her hand, three tasks had
to be completed. But anyone who
failed would lose their head.
Joseph had seen the Princess and
decided to try.

For the first task the Princess
threw her necklace into the deepest
part of the sea, and he had to get it
back. The sea was very rough and he
knew if he tried to swim he would
drown. As he was deciding what to
do the three fish that he had saved
swam up to him with the necklace.

The second task was even
more difficult than the first. Joseph
had to pick up one thousand grass
seeds that the Princess had
scattered in the garden. As

he started picking up the seeds the
ants appeared each carrying a grass
seed. They found every single seed
and placed them in Joseph's bag.

The last task seemed impossible,
Joseph had to find a rose bush that
went from seed to full flower in one
day. Just as he was thinking he
would have to tell the King that
he had failed he saw the three
small ravens carrying a tiny
rose bush between them.
They had found the rose
bush in an enchanted
garden belonging to a witch.

Joseph had completed
all three tasks! He took
the hand of the Princess
and they were married.

Goldilocks and
the Three Bears

Once upon a time there was a little girl called
Goldilocks. Her mother warned her never
to wander into the forest, in case she
got lost. Goldilocks did not always
do as she was told.

One day, when she was
sure her mother wasn't watching,
she ran quickly down the path to
the forest, certain that she would be
able to find her way home.

She wandered happily in the
forest looking at the birds and
flowers. Soon she was tired

and turned to go home but realised she was lost, then she began to cry. Still crying, Goldilocks carried on walking until she saw a tiny cottage in a clearing. Drying her eyes, she crept towards the cottage, knocked on the door and looked through the windows. There was no-one home, so she opened the door and went in.

Inside the cottage everything looked very comfortable. On the table she saw three bowls of porridge – a big one, a middle-sized one and a small one.

She was very hungry and tried the big bowl
but it was too hot. She tried the next bowl but
that was too cold. Then she tried the small bowl,
it was just right and she ate all the porridge.

By the fire were three chairs – a big one,
a middle-sized one and a small one. Goldilocks
tried the big chair but that was too high. So she
tried the middle-sized one but that was too hard.
When she tried the small one she found it was
just right but it broke as she sat on it.

Then she went upstairs where
there were three beds – a big one,
a middle-sized one and a small
one. She tried the big bed
but it was too hard.
She tried the
middle-sized bed

but it was too soft. The small one was just
right, and she soon fell fast asleep.

The cottage belonged to three bears and
when they got home, Father Bear growled,
"Who has been eating my porridge?"
"Who has been eating my porridge?" said
Mother Bear in her gentle voice.

"Who has been eating my porridge
and eaten it all up?" cried
Baby Bear in his squeaky
little voice.

Then Father Bear
saw his chair,
"Who has been
sitting in my
chair?"
"Who has been
sitting in my
chair?" said
Mother Bear in her
gentle voice.
"Who has been sitting in my chair and
broken it?" cried Baby Bear in his squeaky
voice.

Next they went upstairs.
"Who has been sleeping in my bed?"
growled Father Bear.
"Who has been sleeping
in my bed?" said
Mother Bear.

"Who is this, fast asleep in my bed?"
cried Baby Bear.
"She ate all my porridge and she
broke my chair," wailed Baby Bear.
Suddenly Goldilocks woke up,
"Oh, my!" she screamed and,
jumping out of bed, ran across
the bedroom, down the stairs and
out of the door before the bears
could follow her. She ran and ran,
down the path, across the clearing
and through the trees, until she
arrived home.
    Goldilocks never went
wandering alone in
    the forest again.